The Glow of Us

Callum Dettmann

Contents

Chapter 1

The morning sun cast a warm glow over the serene campus of Serenity Springs University as Valentina Parker strolled through the familiar pathways. Memories of her childhood friend, Aziel Mitchell, danced at the edge of her consciousness, invoking a bittersweet longing.

Lost in thought, Valentina rounded a corner and nearly collided with a figure hurrying in the opposite direction. With a gasp, she recognized Aziel – his unruly curls and infectious grin unchanged.

"Aziel?" Valentina's voice wavered with disbelief.

Surprised, Aziel halted, his eyes widening in recognition. "Valentina? Is that really you?"

A rush of emotion flooded Valentina as they embraced, the years melting away in an instant. "It's really you," she murmured.

Aziel chuckled, his laughter breaking the silence of the morning. "Of course it's me. Who else would it be?"

As they parted, Valentina felt a sense of belonging she hadn't known in years. "It's been too long," she admitted softly.

Aziel nodded, mirroring her sentiment. "Way too long. But we're here now, right?"

Valentina smiled, warmth spreading through her chest. "Yeah, we're here now. Let's catch up tomorrow?"

Aziel's grin widened. "Absolutely! Can't wait."

As they went their separate ways, Valentina felt a spark of hope. Maybe this unexpected reunion was the start of something wonderful.

The next day, Valentina found herself sitting across from Aziel in a cozy café nestled in the heart of the city. The aroma of freshly brewed coffee filled the air, and soft jazz music played in the background, creating the perfect ambiance for their reunion.

"So, tell me, Val," Aziel began, his eyes bright with anticipation. "What have you been up to all these years?"

Valentina smiled, grateful for the chance to reconnect. "Well, after high school, I took a gap year to travel a bit. Then, I decided to major in journalism here at Serenity Springs."

Aziel's eyebrows shot up in surprise. "Journalism, huh? That's awesome! Always knew you had a way with words."

The compliment warmed Valentina's heart, and she couldn't help but return the sentiment. "And what about you, Aziel? What have you been doing?"

Aziel scratched the back of his head, a sheepish grin spreading across his face. "Well, after my family moved away, I spent a few years figuring things out. But now, I'm back, studying environmental science."

Valentina nodded, impressed. "That sounds like a perfect fit for you, Aziel. You always did have a passion for nature."

Their conversation flowed effortlessly, punctuated by shared laughter and fond reminiscences of their childhood adventures. With each passing moment, Valentina felt the walls around her heart begin to crumble, replaced by a sense of ease and comfort in Aziel's presence.

As they finished their coffee, Valentina couldn't help but feel a sense of gratitude for the unexpected reunion that had brought them back together. Maybe, just maybe, Serenity Springs held more than just memories of the past – perhaps it held the promise of a bright future, filled with friendship, laughter, and maybe even love.

Chapter 2

The aroma of freshly brewed coffee enveloped Valentina and Aziel as they sat in the cozy café downtown. Soft jazz music played in the background, creating a soothing atmosphere that seemed to invite heartfelt conversations. With each sip of coffee, memories of their shared past flooded back, weaving a tapestry of nostalgia and warmth.

"So, Val," Aziel began, leaning back in his chair with a contented smile, "tell me more about your adventures during your gap year. I'm dying to hear all about it."

Valentina's eyes sparkled with excitement as she recalled her travels. "Oh, Aziel, it was incredible. I traveled to Europe, backpacking through ancient cities and exploring hidden gems off the beaten path. I visited museums, hiked through picturesque landscapes, and met people from all walks of life. It was truly a transformative experience."

Aziel listened intently, hanging onto her every word. "Wow, that sounds amazing," he exclaimed, genuine admiration in his voice. "I've always wanted to travel like that, to immerse myself in different cultures and see the world through new eyes. Maybe one day I'll get the chance."

Valentina smiled warmly, her heart swelling with affection for her childhood friend. "You would love it, Aziel. You have such a curious spirit and an open heart. I have no doubt you'd thrive in any adventure you embark on."

As they continued to chat, their conversation meandered through topics both lighthearted and profound. They talked about their favorite childhood memories - summers spent chasing fireflies, secret hideouts in the woods, and late-night stargazing sessions that seemed to stretch on for eternity.

But amidst the laughter and reminiscing, there was also a palpable sense of vulnerability, a willingness to share their hopes, dreams, and fears. Valentina opened up about her struggles with self-doubt and insecurity, admitting that she often felt lost in the vast expanse of the world.

Aziel listened attentively, his gaze softening with empathy. "Val, you're stronger than you think," he reassured her, reaching across the table to squeeze her hand gently. "You have a fire within you, a passion for life that shines brighter than any star in the night sky. Don't ever let anyone dim that light."

Valentina's eyes brimmed with tears at his words, touched by his unwavering support. In that moment, she felt a deep sense of gratitude for the friendship they shared - a friendship that had weathered the storms of time and distance, emerging stronger and more resilient than ever.

As the afternoon sun began to dip below the horizon, casting a warm glow over the café, Valentina and Aziel realized with a start that hours had flown by in the blink of an eye. Reluctantly, they bid each other farewell, promising to meet again soon.

As Valentina made her way back to her dorm, her heart felt lighter than it had in ages. She couldn't shake the feeling that maybe, just maybe, this unexpected reunion with Aziel was exactly what she needed to find her way in the world.

And as she drifted off to sleep that night, memories of their conversation danced through her mind, filling her dreams with visions of possibility and promise. For the first time in a long time, Valentina felt hopeful about the future, knowing that no matter what challenges lay ahead, she had a friend by her side who believed in her with unwavering faith.

Chapter 3

The next morning, Valentina awoke with a sense of anticipation coursing through her veins. The unexpected reunion with Aziel had left her feeling invigorated, and she couldn't wait to see him again. As she got ready for the day ahead, her mind buzzed with thoughts of their conversation and the promise of new adventures to come.

Heading out of her dorm, Valentina decided to stop by the campus bookstore before meeting Aziel. As she browsed through the shelves, a small slip of paper caught her eye. It was wedged between two books, as if it had been deliberately hidden there.

Curiosity piqued, Valentina carefully extracted the slip of paper and unfolded it. On it was a handwritten message, simple yet cryptic:

"Follow the path where memories intertwine, Seek the truth beneath the stars that shine."

Confusion furrowed Valentina's brow as she read the enigmatic words. Who had left this note for her, and what did it mean? The mention of memories and stars stirred something deep within her, igniting a spark of curiosity.

With a sense of determination, Valentina decided to follow the clues and uncover the mystery behind the note. Perhaps it was a playful prank, or maybe it held a deeper significance that she had yet to understand.

Pocketing the note, Valentina made her way to the café where she was supposed to meet Aziel. As she walked, her mind raced with possibilities, each one more fantastical than the last. But amidst the excitement, a nagging doubt lingered – was she chasing after something real, or simply grasping at shadows?

Arriving at the café, Valentina spotted Aziel waiting for her at their usual table. His bright smile and easy demeanor instantly put her at ease, banishing her doubts and fears. Pushing aside thoughts of the mysterious note for now, Valentina greeted Aziel with a warm hug, eager to immerse herself in his company once more.

As they settled into their conversation, Valentina found herself sharing snippets of her morning adventure with Aziel, including the discovery of the cryptic note. Intrigued, Aziel listened intently, his eyes sparkling with curiosity.

"A mysterious note, huh?" he mused, a playful grin tugging at the corners of his lips. "Sounds like the beginning of an adventure."

Valentina couldn't help but laugh at his infectious enthusiasm. "I suppose it does," she replied, a smile tugging at her own lips. "Who knows what secrets it might hold?"

As they continued to chat, the mystery of the note faded into the background, replaced by the easy rhythm of their conversation. Yet, in the back of Valentina's mind, the words lingered, a tantalizing promise of something yet to come.

Little did she know, this mysterious note was just the beginning of a journey that would take her to places she never imagined, and reveal secrets hidden beneath the surface of her own past.

Days passed since Valentina discovered the mysterious note, yet its words continued to linger in her thoughts like a haunting melody. She couldn't shake the feeling that there was something significant hidden within those cryptic lines, something waiting to be uncovered.

One evening, as Valentina sat alone in her dorm room, she found herself drawn to the note once again. Retrieving it from her bedside table, she studied the words intently, searching for any clue that might shed light on its meaning.

"Follow the path where memories intertwine, Seek the truth beneath the stars that shine."

The words echoed in her mind, stirring a sense of restlessness within her. What path was she meant to follow, and what truth lay beneath the stars? Determined to find answers, Valentina resolved to delve deeper into the mystery.

With a sense of purpose, Valentina set out into the night, her footsteps guided by the faint glow of streetlights overhead. She wandered through the quiet streets of the campus, lost in thought as she retraced the steps of her past.

As she walked, fragments of memories resurfaced – moments shared with Aziel, laughter echoing through the corridors of time. Each memory was like a piece of a puzzle, waiting to be fitted together to reveal the bigger picture.

Suddenly, Valentina's attention was drawn to a familiar landmark – a secluded garden tucked away behind the university's main building. It was a place she and Aziel often visited during their childhood, a sanctuary where they would spend hours lost in conversation or simply enjoying each other's company.

With a sense of anticipation, Valentina made her way to the garden, her heart pounding with excitement. As she stepped through the wrought iron gate, she felt a rush of nostalgia wash over her, mingling with the cool night air.

The garden was bathed in moonlight, casting long shadows across the lush greenery. Valentina took a moment to soak in the beauty of her surroundings, the tranquility of the night enveloping her like a comforting embrace.

And then, she saw it – a glimmer of light shining from the base of an ancient oak tree at the center of the garden. With a sense of trepidation, Valentina approached, her footsteps muffled by the soft carpet of grass beneath her feet.

Beneath the tree, she found a small wooden box nestled among the roots, its lid slightly ajar as if waiting to be opened. With trembling hands, Valentina reached out and lifted the lid, revealing its contents.

Inside the box, she found a collection of old photographs – snapshots of her and Aziel from their childhood, frozen in time like fragments of a forgotten dream. Each photograph held a precious memory, a glimpse into the bond they shared.

As Valentina flipped through the photographs, her heart swelled with emotion. Here they were, captured in moments of pure joy and innocence, their smiles shining bright against the backdrop of their youth.

And then, nestled among the photographs, Valentina found another note – this one written in Aziel's hand-writing, his words filled with warmth and affection.

"Valentina," the note read, "I hope these memories bring you as much joy as they've brought me. No matter where life takes us, know that you'll always have a special place in my heart. Thank you for being my friend, my confidante, and my sunshine on even the darkest days."

Tears welled up in Valentina's eyes as she read the note, overwhelmed by the depth of emotion in Aziel's words. In that moment, she realized that the true treasure wasn't the photographs or the notes – it was the bond they shared, a bond that transcended time and distance.

With a smile on her lips and warmth in her heart, Valentina closed the lid of the box and tucked it safely beneath the tree. As she made her way back to her dorm, she knew that she had found the answers she sought – not in the mystery of the note, but in the whispers of the past.

And as she drifted off to sleep that night, surrounded by memories old and new, Valentina felt a profound sense of gratitude for the journey that had led her here

– a journey of friendship, love, and the enduring power of connection.

Chapter 4

As the weeks passed, Valentina and Aziel's quest to unravel the mystery of the cryptic note led them down a winding path of discovery. They scoured the campus for hidden clues, delving into forgotten archives and dusty old books in search of answers.

One chilly afternoon, while exploring the university's historical archives, Valentina stumbled upon an old photograph tucked away in a dusty corner. It depicted a group of students gathered around a statue - a statue that bore a striking resemblance to the one described in the cryptic note.

Excitedly, Valentina called Aziel over, her fingers trembling with anticipation as she pointed to the photograph. "Look, Aziel! This statue...it's the same one mentioned in the note."

Aziel's eyes widened in surprise as he examined the photograph. "You're right," he exclaimed, his voice filled with wonder. "But what does it mean? And who are these people?"

Valentina studied the photograph intently, her mind racing with possibilities. "Perhaps they were students here at Serenity Springs," she mused. "Maybe they knew something about the statue - something that could help us uncover the truth."

Determined to learn more, Valentina and Aziel set out to track down the individuals in the photograph. They scoured old yearbooks and alumni records, piecing together the identities of the students depicted in the faded image.

Their search led them to a retired professor who had once taught at the university. With a mix of trepidation and excitement, Valentina and Aziel arranged to meet with him, hoping he could shed light on the mystery that had consumed their thoughts for weeks.

As they sat across from the elderly professor in his cozy study, Valentina and Aziel recounted their journey - from the discovery of the cryptic note to the photograph hidden in the archives. The professor listened intently, his eyes shining with a wisdom born of years of experience.

When they finished, the professor leaned back in his chair, a thoughtful expression on his weathered face. "My dear students," he began, his voice tinged with nostalgia, "what you seek is more than just a mere puzzle to be solved. It is a journey into the heart of Serenity Springs - a journey that will reveal secrets long buried beneath the surface."

With that cryptic statement, the professor reached into a drawer and pulled out a weathered journal. "This belonged to one of the students in the photograph," he explained, handing it to Valentina. "Perhaps it holds the answers you seek."

Valentina's hands shook with anticipation as she opened the journal, her eyes scanning the faded pages for any clue that might unlock the mystery of the cryptic note. And as she read the words written by a long-forgotten student, she felt a sense of connection - a connection to the past that would shape the course of their journey in ways they could never have imagined.

Valentina's heart raced as she read through the pages of the weathered journal, each word unveiling a new layer of the mystery surrounding the cryptic note. The journal belonged to a student named Amelia Sinclair, who had attended Serenity Springs University decades ago. Her entries chronicled her experiences as a member of a secret society known as the "Guardians of Serenity."

According to Amelia's writings, the Guardians were dedicated to preserving the history and traditions of the university, guarding its secrets from those who sought to exploit them for personal gain. The statue mentioned in the cryptic note was a significant symbol to the Guardians, believed to hold the key to unlocking the university's most closely guarded secrets.

Excitement bubbled within Valentina as she shared the contents of the journal with Aziel and the retired professor. Together, they pieced together the clues hidden within Amelia's writings, determined to uncover the truth behind the statue and its significance to the Guardians.

Their research led them to a secluded courtyard on the outskirts of campus, where the statue stood tall and imposing against the backdrop of towering trees. As they approached, Valentina felt a sense of reverence wash over her, as if the statue held a power beyond comprehension.

With trembling hands, Valentina reached out to touch the statue's weathered surface, tracing the intricate carvings that adorned its base. As her fingers brushed against the stone, she felt a surge of energy course through her, as if the statue itself was alive with ancient magic.

Suddenly, a hidden compartment within the statue's base caught Valentina's eye. With a sense of anticipation, she reached inside and pulled out a small, ornately decorated box. Inside, nestled among velvet cushions, lay a single object - a shimmering crystal pendant.

A sense of awe washed over Valentina as she gazed at the pendant, its facets catching the sunlight and refracting it into a dazzling array of colors. It was unlike anything she had ever seen before, its beauty both mesmerizing and intoxicating.

As she held the pendant in her hand, Valentina felt a connection to something greater than herself - a connection to the legacy of the Guardians and the secrets they had sworn to protect. And in that moment, she knew that their journey was far from over.

With the pendant clutched tightly in her hand, Valentina turned to Aziel and the retired professor, her eyes shining with determination. "We may have uncovered the first piece of the puzzle," she said, her voice filled with conviction, "but there is still so much more to discover. Together, we will unlock the secrets of Serenity Springs and uncover the truth hidden beneath its hallowed halls."

With renewed purpose, Valentina and her companions set out to unravel the mysteries that lay ahead, their hearts filled with hope and their spirits ablaze with the promise of adventure.

Little did they know, their quest would lead them to the very heart of Serenity Springs, where the truth awaited them - a truth that would forever change the course of their lives and the destiny of the university itself.

Chapter 5

As Valentina, Aziel, and the retired professor delved deeper into their investigation, shadows of doubt began to creep into their minds. The discovery of the pendant had only deepened the mystery surrounding the Guardians of Serenity and their enigmatic purpose. With each step they took, they found themselves treading on increasingly uncertain ground.

Their research led them to the university's archives once more, where they pored over ancient texts and forgotten manuscripts in search of any mention of the Guardians. But the further they delved, the more elusive the truth seemed to become, slipping through their fingers like grains of sand.

Frustration gnawed at Valentina's resolve as she sifted through yet another dusty tome, her eyes scanning the pages for any clue that might lead them closer to the answers they sought. But try as she might, the words remained cryptic, their meaning shrouded in mystery.

Aziel's typically jovial demeanor had grown somber, his brow furrowed with worry as he wrestled with the weight of their quest. "What if we're chasing after something that doesn't exist?" he wondered aloud, his voice tinged with uncertainty.

The retired professor, too, seemed troubled by their lack of progress, his normally sharp mind clouded by doubt. "Perhaps we've been chasing shadows all along," he mused, his tone tinged with resignation. "Or perhaps the truth we seek is buried deeper than we could ever imagine."

Valentina felt a pang of disappointment at their words, her heart heavy with uncertainty. Had their quest been in vain? Were they chasing after a fantasy, doomed to wander in the darkness forever?

But even in the face of doubt, Valentina refused to give up hope. She had come too far to turn back now, her determination unshakeable in the face of adversity. "We can't give up," she insisted, her voice ringing with conviction. "There's still more to uncover – I can feel it."

With renewed determination, Valentina and her companions resolved to press on, their spirits undaunted by the challenges that lay ahead. Though the path ahead was shrouded in darkness, they knew that with perseverance and courage, they would eventually find the light.

And so, they set out once more, their hearts filled with hope and their minds ablaze with the promise of discovery. For even in the darkest of times, the spark of curiosity and the flame of determination could illuminate even the deepest shadows.

Little did they know, their journey was far from over, and the greatest challenges still lay ahead.

As Valentina and Aziel continued their quest to unravel the mysteries surrounding the Guardians of Serenity, their bond grew stronger with each passing day. Amidst the challenges and uncertainties they faced, their friendship blossomed into something deeper – a connection that transcended time and space.

One evening, as they sat beneath the stars in a secluded corner of the campus, Valentina and Aziel found themselves drawn into an intimate conversation that seemed to dance on the edge of something more. The air was filled with the soft murmur of the night breeze, and the moon cast a gentle glow upon their faces as they spoke.

"Valentina," Aziel began, his voice barely above a whisper, "there's something I've been meaning to tell you."

Valentina's heart skipped a beat at the earnestness in his tone, her breath catching in her throat. "What is it, Aziel?" she asked, her voice barely more than a whisper.

Aziel's gaze met hers, his eyes shining with a warmth that set her heart ablaze. "I've known you for as long as I can remember, Val," he confessed, his voice tinged with emotion. "And in all that time, I've never met anyone quite like you. You're like a ray of sunshine on even the darkest of days, and I... I can't imagine my life without you."

Tears welled up in Valentina's eyes at his words, her heart overflowing with a love she had long kept hidden. "Aziel," she murmured, reaching out to touch his hand, "you have no idea what your friendship means to me. You've been my rock through all of this, and I... I'm so grateful to have you in my life."

In that moment, the world seemed to fade away, leaving only the two of them suspended in time. And as they gazed into each other's eyes, a silent understanding passed between them – a promise of something more, waiting to be explored.

With a tenderness born of years of shared experiences, Aziel reached out and brushed a stray lock of hair from Valentina's face, his touch sending shivers down her spine. "Valentina," he whispered, his voice barely audible above the rustle of the leaves, "I... I think I'm falling in love with you."

Valentina's heart soared at his words, her soul singing with a joy she had never known. "Oh, Aziel," she breathed, her voice trembling with emotion, "I think I'm falling in love with you too."

And in that moment, beneath the canopy of stars, Valentina and Aziel's friendship blossomed into something more – a love that would withstand the tests of time and the trials of fate. For in each other's arms, they found solace, strength, and a love that would light their way through even the darkest of nights.

Chapter 6

As Valentina and Aziel's relationship blossomed into a romance filled with promise and affection, their determination to unravel the mystery of the Guardians of Serenity only grew stronger. With newfound resolve and a renewed sense of purpose, they delved deeper into their investigation, determined to unlock the secrets hidden within the heart of Serenity Springs University.

Their search led them to the university's ancient library, a labyrinth of books and knowledge that held the key to unlocking the secrets of the past. Guided by the clues they had uncovered so far, they combed through dusty tomes and ancient scrolls, searching for any mention of the Guardians and their elusive purpose.

Hours turned into days as they poured over the library's vast collection of texts, their determination unwavering despite the countless dead ends they encountered. But just when they were on the brink of giving up hope, a glimmer of light pierced the darkness – a reference to a hidden chamber beneath the university, rumored to hold the answers they sought.

Excitement bubbled within Valentina and Aziel as they pieced together the clues that would lead them to the hidden chamber. With each new discovery, they felt themselves drawing closer to the truth – a truth that had remained hidden for centuries, waiting to be uncovered by those brave enough to seek it.

Their journey took them deep beneath the earth, into the labyrinthine tunnels that lay hidden beneath the university's foundations. Guided by the light of their shared determination and the flickering glow of torches, they pressed onward, their hearts pounding with anticipation.

"And here we are, Val," Aziel whispered, his voice echoing softly in the dimly lit tunnel. "Closer than ever to finding out what this is all about."

Valentina nodded, her heart racing with excitement. "I can't believe we're finally here, Aziel," she replied, her voice filled with awe. "It's like something out of a storybook."

With each step they took, the anticipation grew, until at last they reached the entrance to the hidden chamber. With trembling hands, Valentina and Aziel pushed open the heavy stone door, revealing a sight that took their breath away.

"Incredible," Valentina breathed, her eyes wide with wonder as she took in the sight before her.

Aziel nodded in agreement, his gaze sweeping over the chamber's ancient walls. "It's like stepping back in time," he murmured, his voice filled with reverence.

As they approached the pedestal at the center of the chamber, Valentina's heart pounded with excitement. With trembling hands, she reached out and opened the small, ornately decorated chest, revealing the ancient artifacts within.

Among the artifacts was a scroll, its edges yellowed with age and its ink faded with time. With bated breath, Valentina unrolled the scroll, her eyes scanning the words inscribed upon its surface.

"What does it say?" Aziel asked, his voice filled with anticipation.

Valentina's eyes widened as she read the ancient text, her voice barely above a whisper. "It's a message from the Guardians," she replied, her voice tinged with awe. "They knew we would come, Aziel. They've been waiting for us."

And as Valentina and Aziel gazed upon the ancient scroll, a sense of wonder filled their hearts. For in that moment, they realized that their journey was far from over.Valentina and Aziel sat in the dimly lit chamber, the ancient scroll spread out before them, its words shimmering with a sense of importance. As they read through the message left by the Guardians of Serenity, a sense of reverence filled the air, as if they were in the presence of something sacred.

"These words... they speak of a legacy," Valentina whispered, her voice filled with wonder. "A duty passed down through generations, entrusted to those deemed worthy of carrying on the Guardians' mission."

Aziel nodded, his eyes alight with excitement. "It's like we're a part of something bigger than ourselves," he mused, his gaze fixed on the ancient text. "A legacy that spans centuries, connecting us to those who came before us."

As they continued to read, the message began to unfold a tale of ancient guardianship, tasked with protecting the university and its secrets from those who would seek to exploit them for personal gain. The Guardians had sworn an oath to uphold the values of knowledge, wisdom, and integrity, ensuring that Serenity Springs remained a beacon of enlightenment for generations to come.

"But why us?" Aziel wondered aloud, his brow furrowed with uncertainty. "Why were we chosen to uncover this truth?"

Valentina reached out and squeezed his hand reassuringly. "Perhaps it's because we share the same values as the Guardians," she suggested, her voice filled with conviction. "We believe in the power of knowledge, in the importance of preserving the past for future generations. And maybe, just maybe, that's what they saw in us."

With a newfound sense of purpose, Valentina and Aziel vowed to honor the legacy of the Guardians and continue their mission to protect Serenity Springs University. Armed with the knowledge they had uncovered, they set out to share their discoveries with the world, determined to ensure that the university's secrets remained safe from harm.

But as they prepared to leave the chamber, a sudden realization struck Valentina like a bolt of lightning. "Wait," she exclaimed, her eyes widening with excitement. "What if the pendant we found... what if it's more than just a relic? What if it's a key?"

Aziel's eyes lit up with understanding as he grasped the significance of her words. "You mean... it could unlock the door to even more secrets?" he asked, his voice filled with awe.

Valentina nodded eagerly. "It's worth a try," she replied, her heart pounding with excitement. "And who knows what we might find on the other side?"

With renewed determination, Valentina and Aziel set out to unlock the mysteries hidden within the pendant, their hearts filled with anticipation for the adventures that lay ahead. For as they would soon discover, the legacy of the Guardians of Serenity was far from over – it was only just beginning.

Chapter 7

Valentina and Aziel sat cross-legged on the floor of the chamber, the shimmering crystal pendant resting between them. With trembling hands, Valentina reached out and gently grasped the pendant, her fingers tracing its intricate patterns.

"It's now or never," she whispered, her voice barely above a murmur.

Aziel nodded in agreement, his eyes alight with anticipation. "Let's see if this pendant truly is the key to unlocking the next part of our journey," he replied, his voice filled with excitement.

With a deep breath, Valentina closed her eyes and focused her thoughts on the pendant, willing it to reveal its secrets to them. And then, with a flick of her wrist, she pressed down on a small hidden button nestled among the pendant's delicate filigree.

Instantly, the pendant began to glow with a soft, ethereal light, illuminating the chamber with a warm, golden hue. Valentina and Aziel watched in awe as the light grew brighter and brighter, filling the room with its radiant energy.

And then, with a soft click, the chamber began to tremble, the ancient walls vibrating with an otherworldly power. Valentina and Aziel held onto each other tightly as they felt the ground beneath them shift and sway, as if the very earth itself was awakening to their presence.

And then, with a sudden rush of air, the chamber was filled with blinding light, so bright that Valentina and Aziel had to shield their eyes. And when they opened them again, they found themselves standing in a vast, cavernous chamber, its walls adorned with ancient symbols and carvings.

"We did it," Valentina whispered, her voice filled with wonder.

Aziel nodded, his eyes wide with amazement. "We unlocked the next part of our journey," he replied, his voice tinged with excitement.

As they explored the cavern, they discovered ancient artifacts and relics that spoke of a history long forgotten. Each item they uncovered held a piece of the puzzle, a clue that would guide them on their quest to uncover the secrets of Serenity Springs University.

And as they stood in the heart of the chamber, bathed in the glow of the pendant's light, Valentina and Aziel knew that their journey was far from over. For with each step they took, they drew closer to the truth.As Valentina and Aziel explored the cavernous chamber, they marveled at the ancient artifacts that surrounded them. Each item they discovered seemed to whisper of a bygone era, of a time when the Guardians of Serenity walked the halls of the university with purpose and pride.

Among the relics they found was a series of intricate tapestries, each depicting scenes from the history of Serenity Springs. Valentina and Aziel studied the tapestries with fascination, tracing their fingers over the detailed embroidery that told the stories of generations past.

"It's like stepping back in time," Valentina murmured, her voice filled with awe.

Aziel nodded in agreement, his eyes scanning the tapestries with rapt attention. "These tapestries must hold the key to unlocking the secrets of the Guardians," he replied, his voice tinged with excitement.

As they continued to explore, their attention was drawn to a pedestal at the center of the chamber, upon which rested a shimmering crystal orb. Valentina reached out and gently grasped the orb, her fingers tingling with anticipation.

"It's beautiful," she whispered, her voice filled with wonder.

Aziel nodded, his gaze fixed on the orb's radiant glow. "But what does it do?" he wondered aloud.

Before Valentina could reply, the orb began to pulse with a soft, ethereal light, casting shadows on the cavern walls. And then, with a sudden rush of energy, the light coalesced into a swirling vortex of color, forming images and symbols that danced before their eyes.

Valentina and Aziel watched in awe as the images unfolded before them, revealing a prophecy written in the ancient language of the Guardians. As they read the words inscribed upon the orb, a sense of destiny washed over them, as if they were witnessing the fulfillment of a prophecy written long ago.

"The Guardians foretold of a time when darkness would threaten to consume Serenity Springs," Valentina murmured, her voice trembling with emotion. "But they also spoke of a chosen one – a guardian of light who would rise to defend the university and preserve its legacy for future generations."

Aziel nodded, his eyes shining with determination. "That's us," he replied, his voice filled with conviction. "We are the chosen ones, Val. It's up to us to fulfill the prophecy and protect Serenity Springs from the forces of darkness."

With renewed purpose, Valentina and Aziel vowed to honor the legacy of the Guardians and defend the university against any threat that dared to challenge its sanctity. For they knew that their journey was far from over – it was only just beginning.

And as they stood in the heart of the chamber, bathed in the glow of the crystal orb, Valentina and Aziel knew that they were destined for greatness. For they were the guardians of Serenity Springs, and their legacy would endure for generations to come.

Chapter 8

As Valentina and Aziel emerged from the ancient chamber, their hearts brimming with newfound purpose, they found themselves drawn to each other in a tender embrace. The weight of their shared destiny hung in the air, mingling with the warmth of their affection for one another.

Valentina rested her head against Aziel's chest, her fingers tracing soothing circles on his back. "We have a great responsibility ahead of us," she murmured, her voice soft with emotion.

Aziel wrapped his arms around her, holding her close as if to shield her from the uncertainties that lay ahead. "But we'll face it together, Val," he replied, his voice filled with determination. "As long as we have each other, we can overcome anything."

Their embrace lingered for a moment longer, a silent affirmation of the bond that had grown between them.

And then, with a shared glance and a knowing smile, they set out to continue their journey, hand in hand.

As they walked through the campus grounds, bathed in the soft light of the setting sun, Valentina and Aziel found themselves lost in conversation, their words flowing freely as they shared their hopes, dreams, and fears.

"It's hard to believe how much our lives have changed in such a short time," Valentina remarked, her eyes reflecting the colors of the evening sky.

Aziel nodded, his gaze never leaving her face. "But I wouldn't change a single moment of it," he replied, his voice filled with sincerity. "Every step we've taken has brought us closer together, Val. And I wouldn't want to face this journey with anyone else by my side."

Valentina's heart swelled with love at his words, her eyes shining with unshed tears. "I feel the same way, Aziel," she whispered, her voice barely more than a breath. "You mean everything to me."

Their footsteps echoed softly against the cobblestone path as they continued their walk, their hearts intertwined in a bond that could withstand the test of time. And as they watched the sun dip below the horizon, painting the sky in shades of pink and gold, they knew that their love would endure, guiding them through whatever challenges lay ahead.

For in each other's arms, they had found a love that was as timeless as the stars above – a love that would light their way through even the darkest of nights.

As Valentina and Aziel continued their quest to fulfill the prophecy of the Guardians, they found themselves drawn into unexpected alliances that would shape the course of their journey. One such alliance came in the form of a mysterious figure named Lila, whose arrival brought with it a sense of intrigue and possibility.

It was on a crisp autumn day, as the leaves danced in the breeze and the air was filled with the scent of fallen leaves, that Valentina and Aziel first encountered Lila. She appeared seemingly out of nowhere, her presence commanding attention as she approached them with a knowing smile.

"Hello there," Lila greeted them, her voice soft but filled with an unmistakable air of confidence. "I've been following your journey closely, and I believe I can offer my assistance in your quest."

Valentina and Aziel exchanged curious glances, intrigued by the enigmatic stranger who stood before them. "And what exactly do you bring to the table?" Aziel asked, his voice tinged with skepticism.

Lila's smile widened, her eyes twinkling with mischief. "Knowledge," she replied cryptically. "I have information that could prove invaluable to your mission, if you're willing to hear me out."

With a shared glance, Valentina and Aziel nodded, intrigued by the prospect of gaining new insights into their quest. And so, they followed Lila as she led them to a secluded corner of the campus, where they could speak in private.

As they settled onto a bench beneath the shade of a sprawling oak tree, Lila began to share her knowledge of the Guardians and their ancient prophecy. With each word she spoke, Valentina and Aziel felt a sense of excitement building within them, as if they were on the cusp of a breakthrough that would change everything.

But amidst the serious discussions and strategizing, there were moments of lightheartedness and joy – moments when Valentina and Aziel found themselves lost in each other's company, their laughter mingling with the rustle of the leaves and the chirping of the birds.

One such moment came later that evening, as they sat together on the university's rooftop, watching the stars twinkle in the night sky. With the soft glow of moonlight bathing their faces, Valentina and Aziel found themselves drawn into an intimate conversation that seemed to dance on the edge of something more.

"You know," Aziel began, his voice barely above a whisper, "I never imagined I'd find myself on a journey like this. But with you by my side, Val, I feel like anything is possible."

Valentina smiled, her heart fluttering with affection. "I feel the same way, Aziel," she replied, her voice soft but filled with sincerity. "You've brought so much light into my life, and I'm grateful for every moment we've shared together."

And as they gazed into each other's eyes, bathed in the soft glow of moonlight, Valentina and Aziel knew that their love would guide them through whatever challenges lay ahead. For in each other's arms, they had found a love that was as timeless as the stars above – a love that would light their way through even the darkest of nights.

Chapter 9

Valentina and Aziel's journey with Lila continued, each day bringing new challenges and revelations as they delved deeper into the mysteries of the Guardians. Yet amidst the chaos and uncertainty, their bond only grew stronger, their trust in each other unwavering.

One evening, after a long day of searching for clues and deciphering ancient texts, Valentina and Aziel found themselves alone in their shared quarters. The soft glow of candlelight cast a warm, inviting ambiance as they settled onto the plush couch, seeking solace in each other's presence.

As they sat in comfortable silence, Valentina reached out and took Aziel's hand in hers, her touch gentle and reassuring. "It's been a whirlwind of a day," she remarked, her voice soft but filled with affection.

Aziel nodded, his gaze fixed on her face. "But no matter what challenges we face, I know that as long as we're together, we can overcome anything," he replied, his voice tinged with sincerity.

Valentina smiled, her heart swelling with love for the man beside her. "You're my rock, Aziel," she whispered, her voice barely above a murmur. "I don't know where I'd be without you."

Aziel leaned in closer, his eyes searching hers with a tenderness that took her breath away. "And you're my guiding light, Valentina," he murmured, his voice filled with emotion. "You've brought so much joy and warmth into my life, and I'm grateful for every moment we share together."

Their words hung in the air, a silent affirmation of the deep bond that had formed between them. And then, with a shared smile and a knowing glance, they leaned in closer, their lips meeting in a soft, tender kiss.

Time seemed to stand still as they lost themselves in the sweetness of the moment, their hearts beating as one beneath the weight of their shared love. And as they pulled away, their foreheads touching in a silent promise of devotion, they knew that no matter what trials lay ahead, they would face them together – united in love and unwavering in their commitment to each other.

For in each other's arms, they had found a love that was as pure as it was powerful – a love that would light their way through even the darkest of nights.As the days stretched into weeks, the campus of Serenity Springs University buzzed with anticipation as exam season approached. The air was filled with a palpable sense of tension and excitement, as students prepared to put their knowledge to the test and prove themselves worthy of their studies.

For Valentina and Aziel, exam season brought with it a new set of challenges as they juggled their quest to unravel the mysteries of the Guardians with their academic responsibilities. With each passing day, their time became increasingly scarce as they devoted themselves to studying and preparing for their exams.

Amidst the chaos of exam preparations, Valentina and Aziel found solace in each other's company, their shared determination to succeed serving as a source of strength and motivation. Together, they poured over textbooks and lecture notes, quizzing each other on the intricacies of their respective fields of study.

But as the pressure of exams mounted, so too did the strain on their relationship. There were moments of frustration and exhaustion, as they grappled with the demands of their studies while also trying to maintain the momentum of their quest.

One evening, as they sat together in their shared quarters, surrounded by stacks of books and papers, Valentina sighed heavily, her shoulders slumping with fatigue. "I don't know how much more of this I can take," she confessed, her voice tinged with exhaustion.

Aziel reached out and took her hand in his, his touch gentle and reassuring. "I know it's tough, Val," he replied, his voice soft but filled with determination. "But we're almost there. Just a little while longer, and then we can focus all of our energy on uncovering the secrets of the Guardians."

Valentina nodded, a flicker of hope igniting within her tired eyes. "You're right, Aziel," she murmured, her voice filled with gratitude. "I don't know what I'd do without you."

With renewed resolve, Valentina and Aziel threw themselves back into their studies, their determination unwavering in the face of adversity. And as exam day drew nearer, they knew that no matter what challenges lay ahead, they would face them together – united in purpose and bound by love.

For in each other's arms, they had found a love that was as resilient as it was enduring – a love that would carry them through even the toughest of times.

Chapter 10

As the final days before exams dwindled away, the atmosphere on the Serenity Springs University campus crackled with anticipation. The library was filled with students pouring over textbooks and lecture notes, while study groups gathered in every available corner, their voices a low murmur of concentration.

Valentina and Aziel were no exception to the fervor of exam preparation. They spent long hours in the library, poring over their notes and quizzing each other on the material. Despite the mounting pressure, they found comfort in each other's presence, their shared determination propelling them forward.

One evening, as they sat together in the library, surrounded by stacks of books and papers, Valentina let out a weary sigh. "I don't know how much more of this I can take," she confessed, her voice heavy with exhaustion.

Aziel reached out and squeezed her hand, offering her a reassuring smile. "We're almost there, Val," he said, his voice gentle but firm. "Just a little while longer, and then we'll be free to focus on our quest."

Valentina nodded, a glimmer of hope flickering in her tired eyes. "You're right, Aziel," she replied, gratitude lacing her words. "I couldn't have made it this far without you."

With renewed determination, they threw themselves back into their studies, their minds focused on the task at hand. Hours passed in a blur of textbooks and highlighters, until at last, the final day of exams arrived.

As they sat down at their desks, pencils poised and minds sharpened, Valentina and Aziel exchanged a glance filled with determination. They knew that this was their moment to shine, their chance to prove themselves worthy of the knowledge they had acquired.

And as they tackled each question with precision and focus, they drew strength from the knowledge that they were not alone – that they had each other to lean on, no matter what the outcome.

When the final bell rang and exams were over, Valentina and Aziel emerged from the exam hall with a sense of accomplishment and relief. They had faced the trials of exam season head-on and emerged victorious, their bond stronger than ever.

As they walked hand in hand through the campus grounds, bathed in the golden glow of the setting sun, Valentina and Aziel knew that whatever challenges lay ahead, they would face them together – united in purpose and bound by love.

For in each other's arms, they had found a sanctuary from the chaos of the world – a sanctuary that would carry them through even the darkest of times.

With exams behind them, the campus of Serenity Springs University erupted into a cacophony of celebration. Students streamed out of exam halls, their faces lit up with smiles and laughter as they embraced the freedom that awaited them.

For Valentina and Aziel, the end of exams marked a turning point in their journey. With the weight of academic responsibilities lifted from their shoulders, they found themselves with newfound freedom to focus on their quest to unravel the mysteries of the Guardians.

But before they could dive back into their investigation, there was one more task to attend to – celebrating their hard-earned success. And so, they joined their fellow students in the festivities, reveling in the joyous atmosphere that filled the campus.

The evening sky was ablaze with the glow of paper lanterns and twinkling fairy lights as Valentina and Aziel made their way to the university's central courtyard, where a grand celebration was underway. The air was filled with the sounds of music and laughter as students danced and sang, their voices rising in jubilant chorus.

As they joined in the festivities, Valentina and Aziel found themselves swept up in the excitement of the moment, their hearts light with the promise of what lay ahead. They danced beneath the stars, their laughter mingling with the melodies of the night, as they reveled in the joy of being alive.

But amidst the celebrations, there were moments of quiet reflection – moments when Valentina and Aziel found themselves lost in thought, contemplating the journey that had brought them to this point.

"It's hard to believe how far we've come," Valentina remarked, her voice soft with wonder.

Aziel nodded, his gaze fixed on the twinkling stars above. "But we've only just scratched the surface of what's to come," he replied, his voice filled with anticipation. "I can't wait to see where this journey takes us next."

As they watched the stars twinkle in the night sky, Valentina and Aziel felt a sense of peace settle over them – a peace born of the knowledge that no matter what trials lay ahead, they would face them together, united in purpose and bound by love.

For in each other's arms, they had found a sanctuary from the chaos of the world – a sanctuary that would carry them through even the darkest of times.

Chapter 11

With the festivities winding down, the campus gradually returned to a serene calm. The night air was cool and crisp, carrying the scent of freshly fallen leaves and the distant sound of laughter from lingering celebrations. Valentina and Aziel, their hearts full from the joy of the evening, made their way back to their shared quarters.

The room was bathed in the soft, warm glow of lamplight as they entered, shedding their jackets and settling onto the plush couch that had become their favorite spot for quiet moments together. Valentina leaned into Aziel's embrace, her head resting comfortably on his chest as he wrapped his arms around her, holding her close.

"Tonight was perfect," Valentina murmured, her voice a soft whisper in the tranquil room. "It feels so good to finally have some time to relax."

Aziel nodded, his fingers gently tracing patterns on her back. "We deserved it," he replied, his voice equally soft. "After everything we've been through, it was nice to just let go and enjoy ourselves."

They sat in comfortable silence for a while, the steady rhythm of their breathing syncing as they reveled in the simple pleasure of being together. The warmth of Aziel's embrace and the gentle rise and fall of his chest beneath her head made Valentina feel safe and cherished.

As the minutes stretched into a peaceful eternity, Valentina tilted her head up to look at Aziel. "You know," she began, her voice tinged with a hint of mischief, "we never did finish that discussion about the prophecy and what Lila told us."

Aziel chuckled softly, his eyes sparkling with amusement. "Are you saying you want to talk about ancient prophecies while we're cuddling?" he teased.

Valentina laughed, the sound a melodious echo in the quiet room. "Maybe not right now," she admitted, her smile widening. "But we should start planning our next steps soon. We can't afford to lose momentum."

Aziel nodded, his expression turning serious. "You're right, Val. We need to stay focused. Lila mentioned something about an ancient library hidden beneath the university - a place where the Guardians stored their most important knowledge. If we can find it, it could be the key to understanding the full prophecy and our role in it."

Valentina's eyes lit up with determination. "Then that's our next destination," she declared. "We'll find the library and uncover the secrets it holds. Together."

Aziel tightened his embrace, his heart swelling with pride and love for the woman in his arms. "Together," he echoed, his voice filled with unwavering resolve. "No matter what."

As they settled back into their comfortable silence, the promise of their shared journey hanging in the air, Valentina and Aziel found solace in each other's presence. For in this moment, surrounded by the warmth of their love and the certainty of their shared purpose, they felt ready to face whatever challenges lay ahead.

And as they drifted off to sleep, entwined in each other's arms, they knew that their bond - forged in the fires of adversity and strengthened by their unwavering commitment .The next morning, the campus was quiet, a stark contrast to the vibrant celebrations of the previous night. Valentina and Aziel awoke feeling refreshed and resolute, their minds set on the task ahead. They quickly dressed and headed to the university's archives, where they hoped to find clues about the hidden library Lila had mentioned.

The archives were housed in an imposing, ivy-covered building at the edge of campus. Inside, the air was cool and smelled of old books and parchment. Row after row of towering bookshelves stretched out before them, filled with dusty tomes and ancient manuscripts.

"Where do we even begin?" Valentina wondered aloud, her voice echoing softly in the vast, silent space.

Aziel squeezed her hand reassuringly. "Let's start by looking for any references to the Guardians or hidden chambers. There has to be something here that can point us in the right direction."

They spent hours combing through the archives, poring over books and scrolls, taking notes and cross-referencing texts. The search was painstaking, but they were determined. As the afternoon sun streamed through the tall windows, casting long shadows across the floor, Valentina's eyes fell on an old, leather-bound volume tucked away on a high shelf.

"Aziel, look at this," she called, excitement tinging her voice as she carefully pulled the book down and opened it.

The pages were yellowed with age, the ink faded but still legible. As they read through the text, their eyes widened in realization. The book detailed the history of the university's founding and included references to a secret chamber beneath the main building - a chamber said to house the most precious knowledge of the Guardians.

"This is it," Aziel whispered, his eyes shining with determination. "The hidden library. It's real."

Valentina nodded, her heart racing. "We need to find the entrance. According to this, it's hidden in the old chapel. We have to go there."

With the book in hand, they made their way to the old chapel, a centuries-old structure nestled among ancient oaks at the heart of the campus. The chapel was a beautiful, solemn place, its stone walls and stained glass windows bathed in the golden light of the setting sun.

Inside, the air was thick with a sense of reverence and history. Valentina and Aziel moved through the pews and toward the altar, their eyes scanning every surface for clues. It wasn't long before they found what they were looking for - a small, inconspicuous lever hidden beneath a loose floorboard near the altar.

With a deep breath, Aziel pulled the lever. There was a soft rumbling sound, and a section of the floor slid open to reveal a dark, narrow staircase leading down into the depths of the earth.

"This is it," Valentina said, her voice trembling with a mix of excitement and apprehension.

Aziel took her hand, giving it a reassuring squeeze. "We'll face it together, Val. No matter what we find down there, we'll face it together."

With that, they descended into the darkness, their footsteps echoing off the stone walls as they made their way into the hidden chamber. The air grew cooler and damper as they went deeper, and soon they found themselves standing before a heavy wooden door, ancient and imposing.

Taking a deep breath, Valentina pushed the door open. Inside, they were met with a sight that took their breath away - rows upon rows of ancient books and scrolls, all meticulously organized and preserved. The hidden library was vast, stretching out into the darkness beyond the reach of their lantern's light.

"We found it," Aziel whispered, awe in his voice.

Valentina nodded, her eyes wide with wonder. "This is it. The key to understanding the prophecy and our roles as Guardians. We have everything we need right here."

As they stood together in the hidden library, surrounded by the accumulated knowledge of centuries, Valentina and Aziel knew that their journey was far from over. But with each other by their side and the secrets of the Guardians within their grasp, they felt ready to face whatever challenges lay ahead.

For in this hidden sanctuary, they had found not only the answers they sought but also the strength to continue their quest - united in purpose and bound by love.

Chapter 12

The discovery of the hidden library filled Valentina and Aziel with a renewed sense of purpose. They spent hours pouring over the ancient texts, each page revealing more about the Guardians and the prophecy that had brought them together. The library was a treasure trove of knowledge, and they knew it was the key to unlocking their destiny.

One afternoon, as they sat side by side at a large oak table, Aziel carefully turned the pages of a particularly old and fragile manuscript. "This one talks about the trials the Guardians faced to prove their worth," he said, his voice filled with reverence. "It's said that only those who truly understand the balance of power can complete them."

Valentina leaned in closer, her eyes scanning the intricate illustrations and handwritten notes. "It looks like there are three main trials," she mused. "The Trial of

Wisdom, the Trial of Courage, and the Trial of Unity. Each one tests a different aspect of the Guardians' abilities."

Aziel nodded, a thoughtful expression on his face. "If we can pass these trials, we might be able to unlock the full power of the Guardians and finally understand our roles in the prophecy."

As they continued to study the manuscript, Valentina noticed a small, folded piece of parchment tucked between the pages. She carefully unfolded it, revealing a map of the university grounds with several key locations marked.

"Look at this," she said, pointing to the map. "These markings correspond to the locations of the trials. The first one is here, in the old library."

Aziel's eyes lit up with excitement. "Then we need to go there right away. The sooner we start, the sooner we can unlock the secrets of the prophecy."

With the map as their guide, Valentina and Aziel made their way to the old library. The building was tucked away in a quiet corner of the campus, its stone facade weathered by time. Inside, the air was cool and musty, filled with the scent of aged books and forgotten knowledge.

They followed the map to a small, unassuming door at the back of the library. It creaked open to reveal a narrow staircase leading down into the darkness. As they descended, the air grew colder, and the sound of their footsteps echoed off the stone walls.

At the bottom of the staircase, they found themselves in a circular chamber lit by flickering torches. In the center of the room stood a large, ornate pedestal with a book resting on top. The walls were lined with ancient runes and symbols, their meanings lost to time.

"This must be the Trial of Wisdom," Valentina whispered, her voice filled with awe.

Aziel nodded, his eyes fixed on the book. "We need to figure out what the trial entails and how to pass it. Let's start by examining the book."

As they approached the pedestal, the runes on the walls began to glow softly, casting an eerie light over the chamber. Valentina carefully opened the book, revealing pages filled with complex riddles and puzzles.

"It's a test of our intellect and problem-solving skills," she said, her brow furrowing in concentration. "We need to solve these riddles to prove our wisdom."

Aziel stepped closer, his eyes scanning the first riddle. "We can do this, Val. We've faced tougher challenges before, and we've always come out stronger."

Together, they worked through the riddles, their minds sharp and focused. Each solution brought them closer to unlocking the secrets of the trial, and with each success, the runes on the walls glowed brighter.

Hours passed, but they refused to give up. Their determination and teamwork paid off as they finally solved the last riddle. The room was filled with a blinding light, and when it faded, they found themselves standing in front of a large, intricately carved door that had appeared in the wall.

"This must be the entrance to the next trial," Valentina said, her voice filled with anticipation. "We're one step closer to understanding the prophecy."

Aziel reached out and took her hand, giving it a reassuring squeeze. "Together, Val. No matter what we face, we'll do it together."

With their hands entwined and their hearts filled with determination, Valentina and Aziel stepped through the door, ready to face the next challenge in their journey.

For in each other's arms, they had found the strength to overcome any obstacle – and they knew that their love and unity would carry them through whatever trials lay ahead.

As Valentina and Aziel stepped through the carved door, they found themselves in a dimly lit corridor. The air was thick with anticipation, and the faint glow of torches cast long shadows on the stone walls. The path before them seemed to stretch endlessly into darkness, each step echoing in the silence.

Hand in hand, they moved forward, their hearts beating in unison. The map they had found indicated that this corridor would lead them to the second trial—the Trial of Courage.

"Stay close," Aziel whispered, his voice steady. "We'll face whatever comes together."

Valentina nodded, her grip tightening around his hand. "I'm ready," she replied, determination shining in her eyes. "We can do this."

The corridor eventually opened into a vast chamber, its ceiling lost in darkness. In the center of the room stood a massive stone pillar, etched with ancient symbols. Surrounding the pillar were four statues, each depicting a different mythical creature: a dragon, a griffin, a phoenix, and a hydra.

As they approached the pillar, a deep, resonant voice filled the chamber. "Welcome, Guardians. To prove your courage, you must face your greatest fears. Only by conquering them can you proceed."

Valentina and Aziel exchanged a determined glance. They knew this trial would push them to their limits, but they were ready to face it head-on.

The room darkened, and the statues began to glow with an eerie light. Suddenly, the creatures depicted in the statues came to life, their eyes gleaming with an otherworldly fire.

The dragon roared, its fiery breath illuminating the chamber. The griffin spread its wings, its powerful body poised to strike. The phoenix's feathers shimmered with a golden light, and the hydra's multiple heads hissed menacingly.

Valentina felt a chill run down her spine as the creatures advanced, but she refused to back down. She looked at Aziel, her resolve mirrored in his eyes. "We'll face them together," she said firmly.

Aziel nodded, his gaze unwavering. "Together," he echoed.

The first to attack was the dragon, its massive form lunging toward them with terrifying speed. Valentina and Aziel dodged its fiery breath, their movements perfectly synchronized. They had faced danger before, but this was unlike anything they had ever encountered.

Aziel, with his athletic prowess, managed to climb onto the dragon's back, using its scales to propel himself upward. He aimed for the creature's vulnerable spot, delivering a decisive blow that caused the dragon to roar in pain and vanish into thin air.

Meanwhile, Valentina faced the griffin, her mind racing as she remembered her combat training. She moved with agility, dodging the griffin's powerful strikes and using its momentum against it. With a swift and calculated maneuver, she struck the griffin, causing it to dissolve into mist.

The phoenix was next, its radiant feathers glowing with an intense heat. Valentina and Aziel worked together, using their combined strength and strategy to outmaneuver the mythical bird. With a coordinated effort, they subdued the phoenix, watching as it burst into flames and disappeared.

The final challenge was the hydra, its multiple heads striking with deadly precision. Valentina and Aziel knew that defeating the hydra required more than just physical prowess; they needed to outsmart it. They focused on the creature's weak points, delivering simultaneous strikes that caused the hydra to collapse and vanish.

Breathless and victorious, Valentina and Aziel stood in the now-silent chamber, their bodies and minds tested to their limits. The voice returned, its tone approving. "You have proven your courage, Guardians. You may proceed to the final trial."

As the chamber's walls shifted to reveal a new passage, Valentina and Aziel shared a triumphant smile. They had faced their fears and emerged stronger than ever, their bond unbreakable.

"One more trial to go," Aziel said, his voice filled with determination.

Valentina nodded, her heart swelling with pride and love. "We'll face it together," she said.

Hand in hand, they stepped into the new passage, ready to face the final challenge and unlock the full potential of their destiny.

Chapter 13

The new passage led Valentina and Aziel to an expansive underground cavern. Stalactites hung from the ceiling, shimmering in the faint light cast by glowing crystals embedded in the walls. The air was cool and damp, and the sound of dripping water echoed through the cavern.

As they walked deeper into the cavern, they came upon a large, circular platform surrounded by a shallow moat of crystal-clear water. In the center of the platform stood two pedestals, each holding a small, glowing orb.

Valentina and Aziel approached the platform, and as they stepped onto it, a voice resonated through the cavern. "Welcome, Guardians. The final trial, the Trial of Unity, tests the strength of your bond. Only by working together in perfect harmony can you succeed."

The voice faded, and the orbs began to pulse with a rhythmic light. Valentina and Aziel exchanged a determined glance, knowing that this trial would push their teamwork and connection to the limit.

"We've got this," Aziel said confidently, reaching out to take Valentina's hand. "We've faced everything together so far. We can do this too."

Valentina nodded, squeezing his hand. "Together," she echoed.

The pulsing of the orbs intensified, and suddenly, the platform began to shift and rotate. Sections of the floor rose and fell, creating a complex, ever-changing maze. Valentina and Aziel realized that they needed to navigate the maze while keeping in sync with the orbs' light.

They moved as one, their steps perfectly timed with the rhythm of the orbs. The maze tested their communication and trust, requiring them to anticipate each other's movements and support one another through the shifting terrain.

As they progressed, the challenges became more intricate. Walls of light appeared, blocking their path and forcing them to find alternative routes. Valentina's keen sense of direction and Aziel's agility proved invaluable as they navigated the obstacles, their bond growing stronger with each step.

At one point, they reached a section where the floor crumbled beneath their feet, leaving them precariously balanced on narrow ledges. Valentina felt a surge of fear, but Aziel's steady presence reassured her.

"Trust me," he said, his voice calm and encouraging. "We'll get through this."

Valentina took a deep breath, focusing on Aziel's unwavering confidence. Together, they carefully traversed the ledges, their movements synchronized and fluid. With each challenge they overcame, their trust in each other deepened, and they felt an unbreakable unity.

Finally, after what felt like hours of navigating the maze, they reached the center of the platform. The orbs' pulsing light slowed, and the platform stabilized. The voice returned, filled with pride and approval.

"You have proven the strength of your bond, Guardians. Your unity is your greatest power. You are now ready to fulfill your destiny."

The glowing orbs merged into a single, brilliant light that enveloped Valentina and Aziel. They felt a surge of energy, a deep connection to the ancient power of the Guardians. The light faded, leaving them standing on the platform, their hearts full of determination and purpose.

"We did it," Valentina whispered, her eyes shining with emotion.

Aziel nodded, his gaze filled with love and pride. "We did it together."

Hand in hand, they stepped off the platform, ready to face whatever lay ahead. They knew that their journey was far from over, but with the strength of their bond and the power of the Guardians, they felt prepared to confront any challenge.

For in each other's arms, they had found the unity that would carry them through the trials to come and guide them toward their destiny.

After completing the Trial of Unity, Valentina and Aziel found themselves back in the hidden library. The ancient texts and scrolls seemed to hum with energy, as if recognizing their success. They knew it was time to delve deeper into the prophecy and uncover the full extent of their roles as Guardians.

Valentina carefully unrolled a scroll they hadn't examined before. The parchment was delicate, but the writing was clear and precise. As they read, a story began to unfold - a story that connected their present journey to the ancient past.

"In the beginning, the Guardians were chosen to protect the balance between light and dark," Valentina read aloud. "Their unity and strength ensured harmony in the world. But as time passed, the Guardians were betrayed by one of their own, and the balance was shattered."

Aziel listened intently, his brow furrowing with concern. "A betrayal?" he repeated. "Who would betray the Guardians?"

Valentina continued reading, her voice steady. "The traitor sought to harness the power of darkness for their own gain. They unleashed chaos, and the Guardians were forced to seal their powers to prevent further destruction. The prophecy foretells the return of the Guardians - a new generation who will restore balance and protect the world from the encroaching darkness."

The weight of their responsibility settled over them, but they felt a renewed sense of purpose. They had been chosen to restore the balance, to undo the damage caused by the ancient betrayal.

As they pondered their next steps, a soft rustling sound caught their attention. They turned to see Lila entering the library, her expression one of both relief and urgency.

"I've been searching for you," Lila said, her eyes bright with excitement. "I had a vision. The time is drawing near. We must act quickly."

Valentina and Aziel exchanged a determined glance. "What did you see?" Valentina asked, her voice filled with resolve.

Lila took a deep breath, her gaze unwavering. "The darkness is growing stronger. It seeks to consume everything in its path. But I also saw a way to stop it. We need to find the Heart of Light - an artifact that holds the power to restore balance and vanquish the darkness once and for all."

"The Heart of Light," Aziel mused, his mind racing. "Where do we find it?"

Lila's expression grew somber. "The Heart of Light is hidden in the Temple of Aetheria, a sacred place that has been lost to time. We need to locate it and retrieve the artifact before the darkness overwhelms us."

Valentina nodded, her determination unwavering. "Then that's our next mission. We have to find the Temple of Aetheria and the Heart of Light. We'll restore balance and fulfill our destiny."

With their goal clear, Valentina, Aziel, and Lila began their preparations. They gathered supplies, studied maps, and consulted the ancient texts for clues about the temple's location. The hidden library proved invaluable, its vast knowledge guiding them toward their destination.

As they worked, Valentina and Aziel found moments of quiet togetherness, their bond growing even stronger. One evening, as they sat by the fire in their quarters, Aziel reached out to gently brush a strand of hair from Valentina's face.

"We've come so far," he said softly, his eyes filled with love. "I couldn't have done any of this without you."

Valentina smiled, leaning into his touch. "And I couldn't have done it without you," she replied. "We're stronger together."

They shared a tender kiss, the warmth of their love wrapping around them like a comforting blanket. In that moment, they knew that no matter what challenges lay ahead, they would face them side by side.

The following morning, they set out on their journey to find the Temple of Aetheria. The path was treacherous, filled with obstacles and dangers, but their determination never wavered. Along the way, they encountered ancient guardians and solved intricate puzzles, each step bringing them closer to their goal.

As they neared the temple, they felt the presence of the darkness growing stronger. Shadows loomed at the edges of their vision, and an ominous feeling hung in the air. But they pressed on, their hearts filled with the light of their love and unity.

Finally, they reached the entrance to the Temple of Aetheria, its grand arches and intricate carvings a testament to its ancient origins. The air was thick with power, and they knew they were on the brink of a great discovery.

Together, they stepped into the temple, their hearts beating as one. They had faced trials, uncovered secrets, and strengthened their bond. Now, they stood ready to confront the darkness and fulfill their destiny.

For in each other's arms, they had found the courage, wisdom, and unity needed to restore balance to the world. And with the Heart of Light within their grasp, they would shine brighter than ever, their love guiding them through the darkness and into the light.

Chapter 14

The Temple of Aetheria was even more magnificent than Valentina, Aziel, and Lila had imagined. Its towering pillars were adorned with intricate carvings, and its vast hallways echoed with the whispers of ancient magic. As they stepped inside, the air grew thick with energy, and a sense of awe washed over them.

Valentina gazed at the ornate ceiling, its frescoes depicting scenes of light and darkness locked in eternal struggle. "This place is incredible," she whispered, her voice reverberating in the grand chamber.

Aziel nodded, his eyes scanning the walls for clues. "We need to find the Heart of Light quickly. The darkness is closing in."

Lila led the way, her visions guiding their path through the labyrinthine corridors. "The Heart of Light is at the temple's core," she said with certainty. "But the way is fraught with trials. We must remain vigilant."

Their journey through the temple was filled with challenges that tested their unity and resolve. Ancient traps and puzzles guarded the sacred artifact, each one more difficult than the last. But with Lila's guidance and Valentina and Aziel's unwavering bond, they overcame every obstacle.

As they approached the heart of the temple, they encountered a massive door adorned with glowing runes. Valentina stepped forward, her fingers tracing the intricate symbols. "These runes look like a puzzle," she said, her mind racing to decipher their meaning.

Aziel joined her, his eyes narrowing in concentration. "It's a combination lock. We need to find the correct sequence to open the door."

Lila closed her eyes, her brow furrowing in concentration. "I see... I see the past Guardians. They are showing me the way." She began to chant softly, her words a melodic incantation that echoed through the chamber.

The runes began to shift and align, their glow intensifying until the door finally creaked open. The trio stepped inside, their breaths taken away by the sight before them.

At the center of the chamber stood a pedestal, bathed in a radiant light. On the pedestal rested the Heart of Light, a crystal that pulsed with pure, unfiltered energy.

Its glow filled the room, casting shimmering reflections on the walls.

Valentina approached the pedestal, her heart pounding with anticipation. "This is it," she said softly. "The Heart of Light."

Aziel stood beside her, his hand gently resting on her shoulder. "Together," he whispered. "We'll use its power to restore balance."

As Valentina reached out to touch the crystal, the chamber suddenly darkened, and a chilling voice filled the air. "You dare to defy the darkness?"

A figure materialized before them, cloaked in shadows. Its eyes glowed with malevolent intent, and an aura of pure evil radiated from its form. "I am the Guardian of Shadows," the figure hissed. "And you will not succeed."

Valentina and Aziel stood their ground, their resolve unwavering. "We are the Guardians of Light," Valentina declared, her voice strong. "And we will restore balance."

The Guardian of Shadows lunged at them, its form shifting and twisting with dark energy. Valentina and Aziel moved in perfect harmony, their combined strength and unity guiding their actions.

Lila chanted an incantation, her voice steady and powerful. "By the light that binds us, by the unity of our hearts, we banish the darkness and restore the light!"

A brilliant flash of light erupted from the Heart of Light, engulfing the chamber and the Guardian of Shadows. The darkness screamed in agony, its form disintegrating into nothingness.

When the light faded, the chamber was still, and the Heart of Light glowed with a serene radiance. Valentina and Aziel stood victorious, their hearts filled with hope and determination.

Lila approached them, her eyes shining with pride. "You have proven yourselves worthy," she said. "The Heart of Light is yours to wield. Use its power wisely and restore balance to our world."

Valentina and Aziel carefully took the Heart of Light, feeling its warmth and energy flow through them. They knew their journey was far from over, but with the power of the Heart and the strength of their bond, they felt ready to face whatever challenges lay ahead.

With the Heart of Light safely in their possession, Valentina, Aziel, and Lila made their way back to Silverwood University. The journey was arduous, but their spirits were high, buoyed by their recent victory. They knew that their mission was not yet complete, but they felt stronger and more united than ever before.

As they approached the familiar gates of Silverwood, they were greeted by the university's faculty and students. News of their success had spread, and the entire campus buzzed with anticipation and excitement.

Professor Hawthorne, who had been their mentor and guide throughout their journey, stepped forward to welcome them back. "You have done us all proud," he said, his eyes twinkling with pride. "But your work is not yet finished. The darkness still threatens our world, and we must prepare for the final confrontation."

Valentina and Aziel nodded, their resolve unwavering. "We have the Heart of Light," Valentina said, holding up the radiant crystal. "With its power, we can restore balance and banish the darkness once and for all."

Professor Hawthorne led them to the university's central courtyard, where a large, ornate fountain stood. "The fountain is the heart of Silverwood," he explained. "It is connected to the ancient ley lines that run beneath the campus. By placing the Heart of Light within the fountain, you will amplify its power and create a protective barrier around the university."

Valentina and Aziel carefully placed the Heart of Light in the center of the fountain. As it settled into place, the crystal began to glow with an intense, brilliant light. The water in the fountain shimmered and sparkled, and a wave of energy radiated outward, enveloping the entire campus in a protective barrier.

The students and faculty watched in awe as the barrier formed, their faces filled with hope and determination. They knew that this was only the beginning, but they felt confident in their ability to face the challenges ahead.

As the barrier solidified, a sense of calm settled over the campus. Valentina and Aziel stood hand in hand, their hearts filled with love and unity. They knew that their bond was their greatest strength, and that together, they could overcome any obstacle.

But their moment of peace was short-lived. Lila approached them, her expression filled with urgency. "I've had another vision," she said, her voice tense. "The darkness is gathering its forces. They will attack soon, and we must be ready."

Valentina and Aziel exchanged a determined glance. "Then we will fight," Aziel said firmly. "We will protect Silverwood and the Heart of Light."

The next few days were a flurry of activity as the university prepared for the impending battle. Students and faculty worked together, fortifying the campus and training for the fight to come. Valentina and Aziel led the charge, their leadership and determination inspiring everyone around them.

One evening, as the sun set over the campus, Valentina and Aziel found a moment of quiet amidst the chaos.

They stood by the fountain, watching the Heart of Light pulse with energy.

"We've come so far," Valentina said softly, her gaze fixed on the glowing crystal. "But I can't help but feel a sense of dread. The final battle is approaching, and I don't know what will happen."

Aziel gently took her hand, his touch reassuring. "We'll face it together," he said, his voice filled with conviction. "No matter what happens, we'll stand by each other's side."

Valentina smiled, her heart swelling with love. "Together," she echoed.

As they stood there, wrapped in each other's arms, they knew that their love and unity would guide them through the darkness. They were ready to face whatever challenges lay ahead, knowing that their bond was unbreakable.

For in each other's arms, they had found the strength to overcome any obstacle. And with the Heart of Light at their side, they were prepared to restore balance to the world and banish the darkness once and for all.

Chapter 15

The atmosphere at Serenity Springs University was charged with tension. Everyone on campus, from the oldest professors to the youngest students, felt the weight of the impending battle. Valentina, Aziel, and Lila worked tirelessly to ensure that every aspect of their defense was prepared.

The protective barrier created by the Heart of Light shimmered with an ethereal glow, providing a sense of security. Yet, everyone knew it was only a matter of time before the darkness would make its move.

In the days leading up to the battle, Valentina and Aziel spent every moment they could together, drawing strength from each other. They trained side by side, their movements synchronized and their bond unbreakable. Their love had become a beacon of hope for everyone around them.

One afternoon, as they took a brief respite from their preparations, they sat by the fountain where the Heart of Light rested. The crystal's glow was a comforting presence, reminding them of their mission and the power they held.

Valentina sighed, resting her head on Aziel's shoulder. "Do you ever wonder what will happen after all this?" she asked softly.

Aziel wrapped his arm around her, his gaze fixed on the glowing crystal. "All the time," he admitted. "But I know that as long as we're together, we can face anything. We'll rebuild, we'll heal, and we'll make sure that the darkness never threatens our world again."

Valentina smiled, feeling a renewed sense of determination. "You're right. We've come this far, and we won't stop now."

Their moment of peace was interrupted by the arrival of Professor Hawthorne, his expression grave. "The scouts have returned," he said, his voice heavy with urgency. "The darkness is mobilizing its forces. They'll be here by dawn."

Valentina and Aziel exchanged a determined glance. "Then we need to make sure everyone is ready," Aziel said, rising to his feet.

The rest of the day was a whirlwind of final preparations. Valentina, Aziel, and Lila worked with the other students and faculty to fortify their defenses and ensure that everyone knew their roles. The air was filled with a sense of purpose and resolve.

As night fell, the campus was eerily quiet. The protective barrier cast a soft glow over the grounds, and the Heart of Light pulsed with a steady rhythm. Valentina and Aziel stood at the front of the main courtyard, their eyes scanning the horizon for any signs of movement.

Lila joined them, her expression calm but serious. "The darkness is approaching," she said quietly. "We must stay vigilant."

Valentina nodded, her heart pounding with a mixture of fear and determination. "We'll be ready."

As the first light of dawn began to break, a low rumble echoed through the air. The ground trembled beneath their feet, and a dark cloud appeared on the horizon, slowly advancing toward Serenity Springs.

The darkness had arrived.

The students and faculty of Serenity Springs University stood united, their faces illuminated by the glow of the Heart of Light. As the dark cloud drew closer, a palpable sense of anticipation filled the air. Valentina and Aziel took their places at the front lines, their hearts beating in unison.

The ground shook as the darkness advanced, and the air grew thick with tension. From the shadows emerged dark figures, their eyes glowing with malevolent intent. The darkness had brought its army, and the battle was about to begin.

Valentina raised her voice, calling out to the defenders. "Stay strong! Remember why we're fighting. For our home, for each other, and for the light!"

Aziel's voice joined hers, filled with unwavering confidence. "Together, we will prevail!"

The dark army surged forward, but the defenders of Serenity Springs were ready. The first wave of attackers crashed against the protective barrier, but the Heart of Light's power held strong, repelling the darkness with a brilliant flash of light.

Lila stood at the heart of the defenses, her hands raised as she channeled her visions and energy to support the barrier. "We must hold the line," she called out. "Trust in the light and in each other!"

The battle raged on, the defenders fighting with everything they had. Valentina and Aziel moved together, their movements perfectly synchronized as they struck down the dark figures that breached the barrier. Their love and unity gave them strength, and their presence inspired those around them.

As the hours passed, the darkness intensified its assault. Waves of dark energy crashed against the barrier, each one stronger than the last. The defenders fought valiantly, but the strain began to show.

"We can't let them break through," Valentina shouted, her voice filled with determination. "We have to protect the Heart of Light!"

Aziel nodded, his eyes burning with resolve. "We'll hold them off, no matter what."

Just when it seemed like the darkness might overwhelm them, a blinding light erupted from the Heart of Light. The crystal pulsed with incredible energy, sending a shockwave through the battlefield. The dark figures recoiled, their forms disintegrating in the light's intense brilliance.

For a moment, it seemed like the light might prevail. But then, a chilling laugh echoed through the air, and a figure emerged from the shadows. It was the Guardian of Shadows, more powerful and menacing than ever.

"You think you can defeat me with a mere trinket?" the Guardian of Shadows sneered. "I am the embodiment of darkness. Your light is nothing compared to my power."

Valentina and Aziel stood their ground, their hearts filled with determination. "We won't let you win," Valentina declared. "We will protect our world and restore balance."

The Guardian of Shadows lunged at them, its form shifting and twisting with dark energy. Valentina and

Aziel moved together, their unity and love guiding their actions. They fought with everything they had, their hearts burning with the light of their bond.

But the Guardian of Shadows was relentless. Its attacks were fierce and unyielding, and the strain of the battle began to take its toll on Valentina and Aziel. Just when it seemed like they might be overwhelmed, a surge of energy pulsed through the Heart of Light.

The crystal's glow intensified, and a beam of pure light shot forth, striking the Guardian of Shadows. The dark figure screamed in agony, its form disintegrating in the light's searing brilliance.

As the darkness faded, the battlefield fell silent. The defenders of Serenity Springs stood victorious, their faces filled with relief and triumph. Valentina and Aziel collapsed to their knees, their bodies exhausted but their hearts filled with hope.

Lila approached them, her eyes shining with pride. "You did it," she said softly. "You defeated the darkness."

Valentina and Aziel smiled, their hands still clasped together. "We did it together," Aziel said, his voice filled with love.

The campus erupted in cheers, the sound of victory echoing through the air. The battle was over, and the light had prevailed. Valentina and Aziel knew that their journey was far from over, but they felt ready to face whatever challenges lay ahead.

For in each other's arms, they had found the strength to overcome any obstacle. And with the Heart of Light by their side, they were prepared to restore balance to the world and ensure that the darkness would never threaten their home again.

Chapter 16

The morning after the battle was eerily quiet. The once bustling campus of Serenity Springs University lay still, the echoes of the fierce battle lingering in the air. The protective barrier shimmered softly, a testament to the strength and unity that had seen them through the darkest of times.

Valentina awoke in Aziel's arms, her head resting on his chest. The soft rhythm of his heartbeat was a soothing reminder that they had survived. She looked up at his sleeping face, a mixture of exhaustion and peace etched in his features.

"Morning, Sunshine," Aziel murmured, his eyes fluttering open.

Valentina smiled, brushing a stray lock of hair from his forehead. "Morning. We did it, didn't we?"

Aziel nodded, pulling her closer. "We did. But it's not over yet. We still have a lot to rebuild and heal."

They got up and made their way to the central court-yard. The sight of the Heart of Light still glowing in the fountain filled them with a renewed sense of hope. Around them, students and faculty were already beginning the process of cleaning up and repairing the damage.

Professor Hawthorne approached, his face tired but filled with pride. "You both have done more than we could have ever hoped for. The darkness has been vanquished, but we must stay vigilant. There are always new threats on the horizon."

Valentina and Aziel spent the day helping wherever they could, lending their strength and support to the recovery efforts. They worked side by side, their bond growing stronger with every passing moment. As they rebuilt their home, they also began to rebuild their lives, finding solace in each other's presence.

That evening, they gathered with their friends in the great hall. Lila, ever the seer, had a thoughtful look on her face as she gazed into the flames of the large fireplace.

"What's on your mind, Lila?" Aziel asked, handing her a cup of hot tea.

"I can't shake the feeling that this isn't the end," Lila admitted. "The Guardian of Shadows may be gone, but there are still dark forces at play. We need to be prepared for whatever comes next."

Valentina squeezed Aziel's hand, a determined look in her eyes. "We'll face it together. No matter what happens, we'll be ready."

As they sat together, surrounded by their friends and allies, they knew that their journey was far from over. But for now, they took comfort in each other and the strength they had found in their unity.

Days turned into weeks, and the campus of Serenity Springs University slowly returned to its former glory. The students and faculty worked tirelessly to repair the damage and restore a sense of normalcy. But beneath the surface, there was an undercurrent of unease.

Valentina, Aziel, and Lila continued to keep a close eye on the Heart of Light, ensuring that its protective barrier remained strong. One afternoon, as they were studying ancient texts in the library, Professor Hawthorne entered with a grave expression.

"We've received reports of strange occurrences in the surrounding areas," he said, placing a map on the table. "Dark creatures have been spotted, and there are rumors of a new threat emerging."

Valentina's brow furrowed in concern. "Do we know where these creatures are coming from?"

Hawthorne shook his head. "Not yet. But we believe they are being drawn to the Heart of Light. Its power is a beacon, and it's attracting both light and dark forces."

Aziel stood up, his jaw set in determination. "Then we need to find out who or what is behind this. We can't let another darkness rise."

As they planned their next steps, a mysterious figure appeared at the entrance of the library. Cloaked in shadows, their face was obscured, but their presence was undeniable.

"I hear you're looking for answers," the figure said, their voice smooth and enigmatic. "I may have the information you seek."

Valentina exchanged a wary glance with Aziel and Lila. "Who are you?"

The figure stepped forward, revealing a pair of piercing blue eyes beneath the hood. "My name is Elara. I've been tracking these dark forces for some time. They are unlike anything you've faced before."

Elara's arrival added a new layer of complexity to their mission. She claimed to be a former member of an ancient order dedicated to protecting the balance between light and dark. Her knowledge of the dark creatures and their origins was invaluable, but her motives remained unclear.

Over the next few days, Elara shared what she knew with Valentina, Aziel, and Lila. According to her, the dark creatures were being controlled by a powerful entity known as the Shadow Weaver. This entity had the ability to manipulate the darkness and bend it to its will.

"The Shadow Weaver is ancient and cunning," Elara explained. "It seeks to corrupt the Heart of Light and plunge the world into eternal darkness. You must be cautious."

As they delved deeper into the mystery, tensions began to rise. Valentina and Aziel disagreed on how to handle Elara's information, leading to heated arguments and strained relationships.

"We can't trust her blindly," Valentina insisted one evening, her voice filled with frustration. "We don't know anything about her true intentions."

Aziel ran a hand through his hair, trying to remain calm. "We need her knowledge, Val. Without it, we're at a disadvantage. We have to take the risk."

Their disagreement left them both feeling unsettled, but they knew that they had to stay united if they were to succeed. As they prepared for the challenges ahead, they reminded themselves of the strength they had found in each other and the love that had carried them through the darkest of times.

With the new threat looming on the horizon, Valentina and Aziel vowed to face it together, drawing on their bond and the power of the Heart of Light to protect their world from the encroaching darkness.

Chapter 17

The following morning, Valentina and Aziel found themselves deep within the university's archives, guided by the enigmatic Elara. The air was thick with the scent of old parchment and dust, and the dim lighting added to the sense of mystery that surrounded their quest.

Elara led them to a secluded corner of the archive where an ancient tome lay open on a pedestal. "This book contains the history of the Heart of Light," she explained. "It also holds secrets that might help us understand the Shadow Weaver's intentions."

Valentina ran her fingers over the delicate pages, her eyes scanning the intricate illustrations and cryptic text. "What exactly are we looking for?"

"Anything that can tell us more about the Shadow Weaver and how to defeat it," Elara replied. "There are legends that speak of a weapon or a spell capable of nullifying its power."

As they pored over the tome, Aziel found a passage that caught his eye. "Look at this," he said, pointing to a detailed drawing of the Heart of Light surrounded by a protective barrier. "It mentions a ritual that strengthens the Heart's power, making it impervious to dark magic."

Elara nodded, her expression thoughtful. "Yes, but performing the ritual requires a great deal of energy and precise execution. We'll need to gather specific ingredients and perform the ritual at the peak of the lunar cycle."

Valentina glanced at Aziel, a sense of determination welling up inside her. "Then we have no time to waste. We need to gather everything we need and prepare for the ritual."

Over the next few days, Valentina, Aziel, and Elara set out to collect the necessary ingredients. They journeyed to enchanted forests, ancient ruins, and hidden groves, facing numerous challenges along the way. Each obstacle only strengthened their resolve and deepened their bond.

One evening, as they camped under the stars, Aziel turned to Valentina, his eyes filled with admiration. "You're amazing, you know that? The way you handle everything, your strength... I'm in awe of you."

Valentina smiled, a soft blush creeping up her cheeks. "I couldn't do this without you, Aziel. You give me strength and hope."

Their hands found each other in the darkness, and for a moment, the world seemed to stand still. The connection between them was undeniable, and it gave them the courage to face whatever lay ahead.As they returned to Serenity Springs University with the ingredients for the ritual, a palpable tension hung in the air. The atmosphere was charged with uncertainty, and everyone seemed on edge.

Valentina and Aziel gathered their friends and allies in the great hall, explaining the details of the ritual and the importance of its success. However, not everyone was convinced.

"This is too risky," one student argued. "We don't even know if it will work."

"We have to try," Aziel countered, his voice firm. "If we don't, the Shadow Weaver will destroy everything we've fought to protect."

The debate grew heated, with arguments flying back and forth. Valentina felt her frustration mounting as she tried to keep the group focused on their common goal.

"We need to trust each other," she said, her voice rising above the din. "We've come this far because we believed in the power of unity and the light within us. We can't lose sight of that now."

Lila, who had been quietly observing the exchange, finally spoke up. "Valentina is right. We need to stand together. The Heart of Light chose us for a reason. We must have faith in our abilities and our bond."

Reluctantly, the group agreed to proceed with the ritual. But the tension between Valentina and Aziel, who had been so strong together, began to show. The stress of their mission and the constant pressure weighed heavily on them, leading to their first major argument.

"You're not listening to me, Aziel," Valentina said, her voice edged with frustration. "We need to be more cautious. We can't rush into this without considering the consequences."

Aziel sighed, running a hand through his hair. "I know, but we can't afford to hesitate either. Every moment we delay, the Shadow Weaver grows stronger."

Their disagreement left them both feeling unsettled, but they knew that they had to stay united if they were to succeed. They spent the night in separate quarters, each lost in their thoughts and worries.

The next morning, Valentina sought out Aziel, her heart heavy with regret. She found him by the Heart of Light, his expression troubled.

"Aziel," she said softly, approaching him. "I'm sorry. I shouldn't have pushed you away."

Aziel turned to her, his eyes filled with a mix of emotions. "I'm sorry too, Val. We're in this together. We can't let our differences tear us apart."

They embraced, their connection stronger than ever. "We'll find a way," Valentina whispered. "Together."

With their bond reaffirmed, they rejoined their friends, ready to face the challenges ahead. The ritual was their only hope, and they would give everything they had to ensure its success.

Chapter 18

The following days were a whirlwind of activity as Valentina, Aziel, and their friends prepared for the ritual. Despite the lingering tension, everyone worked tirelessly, gathering the final ingredients and fine-tuning the preparations. The peak of the lunar cycle was approaching, and with it, their chance to strengthen the Heart of Light.

One evening, as the sun dipped below the horizon, Valentina and Aziel found a quiet moment alone in the gardens. The air was cool, and the soft glow of fireflies illuminated the space around them. Valentina leaned against a stone bench, her eyes reflecting the flickering light.

"Aziel," she began softly, her voice barely above a whisper. "I've been thinking... about us."

Aziel turned to her, his expression tender. "What about us?"

She took a deep breath, gathering her thoughts. "We've been through so much together. And I know we've had our disagreements, but... I can't imagine going through this without you."

He moved closer, taking her hands in his. "Val, you're the strongest person I know. And I'm here for you, always. We're a team, and we'll face whatever comes our way together."

Tears welled up in her eyes, but they were tears of relief and love. "I'm sorry for doubting you, for pushing you away. I was scared, and I didn't know how to handle it."

Aziel gently wiped away her tears, his touch comforting. "We're all scared, Val. But we have each other, and that's what matters. We'll get through this, and we'll come out stronger on the other side."

Their lips met in a gentle, heartfelt kiss, sealing their promise to stand by each other no matter what. In that moment, all the fear and uncertainty melted away, replaced by a profound sense of unity and love.

The next morning, they gathered with their friends and allies in the great hall, ready to perform the ritual. The ingredients were arranged in a precise pattern around the Heart of Light, and a sense of anticipation filled the air.

Elara stepped forward, her eyes glowing with determination. "This is it. We must channel our energy and focus our intentions on strengthening the Heart. Together, we can do this."

As they began the ritual, a powerful surge of energy filled the room. The Heart of Light pulsed with an intense, radiant glow, and the protective barrier around it shimmered and expanded. Valentina, Aziel, and their friends poured their strength and love into the ritual, their unity creating a force unlike anything they had ever felt.

When the ritual was complete, the Heart of Light blazed with renewed power, its light banishing the shadows that had threatened to consume them. Exhausted but triumphant, they knew they had taken a crucial step in their fight against the Shadow Weaver.

With the ritual successfully completed, the immediate threat seemed to diminish, but the presence of the Shadow Weaver still loomed large in their minds. The Heart of Light was stronger than ever, but they knew their enemy would not rest.

One afternoon, as Valentina, Aziel, and Lila were discussing their next steps, Elara approached with a troubled expression. "There's something I need to tell you," she said, her voice serious. "I've been sensing a presence—someone who may be able to help us, but their intentions are unclear."

Curiosity piqued, they followed Elara to a secluded part of the campus, where a figure stood waiting. The person was cloaked in shadows, their face hidden beneath a hood. As they stepped forward, the hood fell back, revealing a young woman with piercing green eyes and an air of quiet strength.

"I am Seraphina," she introduced herself, her voice calm and measured. "I've been watching you, observing your struggle. I believe I can help you, but you must trust me."

Valentina and Aziel exchanged wary glances. "Why should we trust you?" Valentina asked, her tone guarded.

Seraphina met her gaze evenly. "Because I know what you're up against. The Shadow Weaver is more powerful than you realize, and it will stop at nothing to corrupt the Heart of Light. I have knowledge and skills that can aid you, but you must decide if you're willing to accept my help."

After a tense silence, Aziel spoke up. "We need all the help we can get. If you can truly aid us, then we welcome you."

Seraphina nodded, her expression resolute. "Very well. There is much to do, and little time to waste. The Shadow Weaver's power grows with each passing day."

Over the next few days, Seraphina proved to be an invaluable ally. Her knowledge of ancient spells and protective enchantments strengthened their defenses, and her insights into the Shadow Weaver's tactics gave them a crucial advantage.

One evening, as Valentina and Aziel were walking through the campus, Seraphina joined them. "There's something you should know," she began, her tone serious. "The Shadow Weaver is not just seeking to corrupt the Heart of Light. It aims to become the new guardian of darkness, a force that could plunge the world into eternal night."

Valentina felt a chill run down her spine. "How do we stop it?"

Seraphina's gaze was intense. "There is a way, but it requires great sacrifice. The Heart of Light must be protected at all costs, even if it means putting your own lives at risk."

Aziel squared his shoulders, his determination unwavering. "We're prepared to do whatever it takes. We won't let the Shadow Weaver succeed."

As they stood together, united in their resolve, Valentina felt a sense of hope. They had come so far, faced so many challenges, and yet their bond had only grown stronger. With Seraphina's help, they had a chance to defeat the Shadow Weaver and protect the Heart of Light.

Their journey was far from over, but they knew they were not alone. With each other and their friends by their side, they would face whatever came their way, determined to protect their world from the encroaching darkness.

Chapter 19

The preparations for the final confrontation with the Shadow Weaver intensified as the days passed. Serenity Springs University became a hive of activity, with students and faculty working together to fortify their defenses and hone their skills. The Heart of Light, now stronger than ever, was their beacon of hope.

Valentina and Aziel spent their days training with Seraphina, learning new spells and tactics that would be crucial in the upcoming battle. They also took time to strengthen their bond, finding solace in each other's presence amidst the chaos.

One evening, as the sun set over the campus, Valentina and Aziel found themselves in their favorite spot in the gardens. The air was cool, and the scent of blooming flowers filled the air.

"Do you remember the first time we met here?" Aziel asked, a soft smile playing on his lips.

Valentina nodded, her eyes reflecting the golden light of the setting sun. "I do. You were so full of energy, like a burst of sunshine."

Aziel chuckled. "And you were so guarded, like a beautiful but distant frost."

They shared a quiet laugh, the memory of their first meeting bringing a sense of warmth and nostalgia. Despite the challenges they had faced, they had found their way back to each other, stronger and more united than ever.

"Aziel," Valentina said softly, turning to face him. "No matter what happens, I want you to know that I love you. You've brought so much light into my life, and I'm grateful for every moment we've shared."

Aziel's eyes softened, and he took her hands in his. "I love you too, Val. You're my anchor, my strength. We'll get through this together, and we'll build a future where we can be happy and safe."

Their lips met in a tender kiss, a promise of love and hope for the future. In that moment, the world around them faded away, leaving only the two of them, connected by a bond that no darkness could ever break.

As they pulled apart, Valentina rested her head on Aziel's shoulder, her heart full of love and determination. They knew the battle ahead would be their greatest challenge yet, but they were ready to face it together.

The night of the final confrontation arrived, and a palpable tension hung in the air. The full moon cast an eerie glow over the campus, illuminating the faces of the students and faculty who had gathered in the great hall. The Heart of Light pulsed with a steady, radiant glow, a beacon of hope amidst the encroaching darkness.

Valentina, Aziel, and Seraphina stood at the front of the hall, addressing the assembled group. "Tonight, we face our greatest challenge," Valentina began, her voice strong and steady. "The Shadow Weaver seeks to corrupt the Heart of Light and plunge our world into darkness. But we will stand together, united in our strength and our love."

Aziel stepped forward, his gaze sweeping over the crowd. "We've trained hard and prepared for this moment. Remember, we are stronger together. Trust in each other, and in the power of the Heart of Light."

Seraphina nodded, her eyes glowing with determination. "Stay focused and stay strong. We have the knowledge and the power to defeat the Shadow Weaver. Let's protect our home and our future."

As the group dispersed to take their positions, Valentina and Aziel shared a moment alone. "Are you ready?" Aziel asked, his voice filled with a mixture of determination and concern.

Valentina nodded, her heart racing. "As ready as I'll ever be. We can do this, Aziel. Together."

They shared a brief, but heartfelt kiss before joining their friends at the Heart of Light. The protective barrier shimmered around them, and a sense of anticipation filled the air.

Suddenly, the ground trembled, and a chilling wind swept through the hall. Shadows began to creep along the walls, twisting and writhing like living entities. The temperature dropped, and an oppressive darkness settled over the room.

The Shadow Weaver had arrived.

A figure emerged from the darkness, cloaked in shadows and exuding a malevolent aura. The room seemed to grow colder and darker with each step it took. "Foolish mortals," the Shadow Weaver hissed, its voice echoing with an otherworldly resonance. "You cannot hope to stop me. The Heart of Light will be mine."

Valentina and Aziel stood their ground, their hands clasped together. "We won't let you succeed," Valentina declared, her voice unwavering. "We will protect the Heart of Light and our home."

The battle began in earnest, with spells and enchantments flying through the air. The students and faculty fought bravely, their combined efforts creating a dazzling display of light and power. But the Shadow Weaver was relentless, its dark magic countering their every move.

Valentina and Aziel fought side by side, their bond giving them strength and focus. They moved in perfect harmony, their attacks complementing each other and creating a formidable force. But despite their best efforts, the Shadow Weaver seemed to grow stronger with each passing moment.

As the battle raged on, Seraphina noticed a pattern in the Shadow Weaver's attacks. "It's drawing power from the shadows around us," she shouted. "We need to cut off its source of strength!"

Valentina and Aziel nodded, understanding the gravity of the situation. They focused their energy on disrupting the Shadow Weaver's connection to the shadows, using their combined power to create bursts of light that shattered the darkness.

The Shadow Weaver shrieked in rage, its form flickering and wavering. "You think you can defeat me?" it snarled. "I am eternal! I am darkness itself!"

But Valentina and Aziel refused to back down. Drawing on the strength of their love and their bond, they unleashed a final, powerful burst of light that engulfed the Shadow Weaver. The darkness shattered, and the creature let out a piercing scream as it was consumed by the light.

When the light finally faded, the Shadow Weaver was gone, and the oppressive darkness lifted. The Heart of Light pulsed with a steady, radiant glow, its power stronger than ever. The room erupted in cheers and cries of relief as the students and faculty celebrated their hard-won victory.

Exhausted but triumphant, Valentina and Aziel embraced, their hearts full of love and hope. "We did it," Aziel whispered, his voice filled with awe and gratitude.

Valentina nodded, tears of joy streaming down her cheeks. "We did it, together."

As they stood in the warm glow of the Heart of Light, surrounded by their friends and allies, they knew that their journey was far from over. But they also knew that they could face anything, as long as they were together.

Epilogue

The days following the battle against the Shadow Weaver were filled with a mixture of relief and reflection. Serenity Springs University began the process of rebuilding, and the atmosphere gradually shifted from one of tension to one of hope.

Valentina and Aziel spent their days helping to restore the campus, using their abilities to mend broken structures and heal those who had been injured. The Heart of Light continued to shine brightly, its presence a constant reminder of their victory and the strength of their bond.

One afternoon, as they worked side by side in the gardens, Aziel turned to Valentina with a thoughtful expression. "Val, there's something I've been thinking about."

Valentina looked up, curiosity in her eyes. "What is it?"

Aziel hesitated for a moment before speaking. "We've been through so much together, and I can't imagine my life without you. I want us to always be together, no matter what the future holds."

A soft smile spread across Valentina's face as she reached out to take his hand. "I feel the same way, Aziel. You're my rock, my light. We've faced so many challenges, but we've always come out stronger."

Aziel squeezed her hand, his eyes filled with determination. "Then let's make a promise to each other. No matter what happens, we'll always support and love each other."

Valentina nodded, her heart swelling with love. "I promise, Aziel. Always."

Their promise solidified their bond even further, and they continued their work with renewed purpose. The campus slowly returned to its former glory, and the sense of community among the students and faculty grew stronger than ever.

As the weeks passed, life at Serenity Springs University began to settle into a new normal. The students resumed their studies, and the faculty focused on creating a safe and supportive environment for everyone. The events of the past months had forged strong connections and a deep sense of unity among the community.

Valentina and Aziel continued to grow closer, their love blossoming in the aftermath of their shared trials. They often found themselves reminiscing about their journey and the moments that had brought them together.

One evening, as they walked hand in hand through the campus gardens, Valentina turned to Aziel with a contemplative look. "Aziel, have you ever thought about what the future holds for us?"

Aziel smiled, his eyes twinkling with affection. "All the time. I see us building a life together, filled with love and adventure. I want to explore the world with you, face new challenges, and create beautiful memories."

Valentina's heart swelled with emotion. "I want that too. We've been through so much, and I know that as long as we're together, we can handle anything."

Their conversation left them both feeling hopeful and excited about the future. They knew that their bond was unbreakable and that they had the strength and love to face whatever came their way.

As the days turned into weeks, Aziel found himself planning something special for Valentina. He wanted to show her just how much she meant to him and to solidify their future together.

One sunny afternoon, Aziel asked Valentina to join him for a picnic in their favorite spot in the gardens.

Valentina agreed, her curiosity piqued by the twinkle in Aziel's eyes.

As they settled on a blanket beneath a large oak tree, Aziel produced a small, intricately wrapped box from his pocket. Valentina's eyes widened in surprise. "Aziel, what's this?"

Aziel took a deep breath, his heart pounding with anticipation. "Val, these past months have been the most incredible journey of my life. You've shown me what it means to truly love and be loved. I want to spend the rest of my life with you."

He opened the box to reveal a beautiful ring, its gemstone sparkling in the sunlight. "Valentina Parker, will you marry me?"

Tears of joy filled Valentina's eyes as she looked at the man she loved. "Yes, Aziel Mitchell, I will marry you!"

Aziel slipped the ring onto her finger, and they shared a passionate kiss, their hearts overflowing with happiness. As they held each other, they knew that this was just the beginning of their new journey together.

The months leading up to Valentina and Aziel's wedding were a whirlwind of excitement and preparation. Their friends and family rallied around them, eager to celebrate their love and support them as they embarked on this new chapter of their lives.

The day of the wedding arrived, and Serenity Springs University was transformed into a scene of pure enchantment. Flowers adorned every corner, and the Heart of Light shone brighter than ever, casting a warm and welcoming glow over the entire campus.

Valentina stood in her dressing room, her heart racing with anticipation. She wore a stunning white gown that flowed gracefully around her, and her hair was adorned with delicate flowers. Lila stood beside her, beaming with pride. "You look absolutely beautiful, Val."

Valentina smiled, her eyes sparkling with happiness. "Thank you, Lila. I'm so grateful to have you by my side."

As the ceremony began, Valentina made her way down the aisle, her heart filled with love and excitement. Aziel stood at the altar, looking dashing in his suit, his eyes locked onto hers with unwavering devotion.

The ceremony was a beautiful blend of tradition and personal touches, reflecting the unique bond that Valentina and Aziel shared. They exchanged heartfelt vows, promising to love and support each other for the rest of their lives.

"I, Aziel, take you, Valentina, to be my wife," Aziel said, his voice filled with emotion. "You are my heart, my light, and my everything. I promise to stand by your side through all of life's challenges and to cherish every moment we share."

Valentina's eyes glistened with tears as she spoke her vows. "I, Valentina, take you, Aziel, to be my husband. You are my rock, my sunshine, and my best friend. I promise to love you unconditionally and to walk beside you on this journey we call life."

As they exchanged rings, a sense of completeness washed over them. The officiant smiled warmly. "By the power vested in me, I now pronounce you husband and wife. You may kiss the bride."

Aziel and Valentina shared a kiss that was filled with love, joy, and the promise of a beautiful future. The crowd erupted in cheers and applause as they walked back down the aisle, hand in hand, ready to face whatever adventures lay ahead.

The reception that followed was a joyous celebration of their love, filled with laughter, dancing, and heartfelt toasts. As the night drew to a close, Valentina and Aziel stole a moment away from the festivities, standing beneath the stars.

"Aziel," Valentina said softly, resting her head on his shoulder. "Today has been perfect. I can't wait to start this new chapter with you."

Aziel wrapped his arms around her, holding her close. "Me neither, Val. Our future is bright, and as long as we're together, I know we can handle anything."

As they stood there, wrapped in each other's embrace, they knew that their love story was just beginning. With the Heart of Light shining brightly within them, they were ready to face the world, hand in hand, forever united by love.